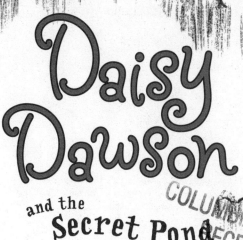

Daisy Dawson

and the
Secret Pond

Steve Voake

illustrated by Jessica Meserve

CANDLEWICK PRESS

For Daisy Voake, with love
S. V.

For Emily
J. M.

Text copyright © 2008 by Steve Voake
Illustrations copyright © 2008 by Jessica Meserve

First U.S. paperback edition 2010

The Library of Congress has cataloged the
hardcover edition as follows:

Library of Congress Catalog Card Number 2008932950

ISBN 978-0-7636-4009-5 (hardcover)
ISBN 978-0-7636-4730-8 (paperback)

17 LSC 10 9 8 7 6

Printed in Crawfordsville, IN, U.S.A.

This book was typeset in StempelSchneidler.
The illustrations were done in ink and pencil.

Candlewick Press
99 Dover Street
Somerville, Massachusetts 02144

visit us at www.candlewick.com

Contents

Chapter 1
Wasps and Chocolate

"Smile, please!" said Daisy as she pressed the button and a bright flash lit up the bathroom. Her dad's foam-covered face froze in the viewfinder, razor held in mid-air and eyebrows raised in surprise.

"Hey!" he protested, scraping another pathway through the foam. "If I'd known we were doing a photo shoot, I'd have dressed up for the occassion."

Daisy reversed into the bedroom, fell backward onto the double bed, and took an action shot of the ceiling on her way down.

"Hey!" said Mom, lifting her coffee cup out of harm's way. "Be careful where you're bouncing, missy!"

"Sorry," said Daisy. "But a good photographer has to be able to take photos on the move." (She had read this in a magazine at the dentist's, so she knew it was true.)

"Like the new camera, then?" asked Dad, toweling his face dry.

"It's the best birthday present ever," said Daisy. She turned around to take a shot of her mom drinking her coffee.

"Well, don't waste the film," said Mom as she flicked through her magazine. "I'm not sure the world is ready for pictures of your dad first thing in the morning."

"Thousands would disagree," said Dad.

"Don't worry," said Daisy. "It's digital. See? You can just delete it if you don't like it." She pressed a button, and the picture

dissolved away
to nothing. "There,"
she said. "All gone!"

Daisy's mom looked at
the clock, then dropped her
magazine and sprang out of bed. "Gone is
where we all should be. It's a quarter past
eight already!"

3

*   *   *

Daisy put her camera back on the shelf and
hoped she wouldn't be late for school again.
Miss Frink had suggested setting her alarm
clock ten minutes earlier, but this just meant
that she had more time to do interesting
things before she left the house.

She picked up the bottle of Strawberry
Surprise (birthday perfume from Grandma)
and squirted some under her chin. It
reminded her of the delicious chewy red
candy she liked so much, so she gave herself
another quick blast. Then she swung her
backpack over her shoulder, jumped down
the stairs three at a time, and ambled into
the kitchen.

"P.U.," said Dad. "What's that smell?"

"It's my perfume," replied Daisy.
"Strawberry Surprise."

"Surprise is right," said Dad, wrinkling up
his nose.

4

"Come on, Daisy," said Mom. "Stop dawdling and get a move on. You know what Miss Frink said about you being late."

"Don't worry, Mom," said Daisy, kissing her on the cheek and skipping out of the back door. "Daisy Dawson is on her way!"

Daisy wandered down the lane, listening
to the bees buzz and the swallows sing.
Apart from a few bumpy white clouds here
and there, the sky was clean and empty.
With the sun warming her face, Daisy leaned
on the gate and gazed at the old tumbledown
barn.

"Boom!" she called. "I've brought you
some breakfast!"

There was a scrabbling sound from inside
the barn, and a large bloodhound
poked its head through
a hole in the wall.

"Morning, Daisy," he said. "You're bright and early."

"Well I *was*," replied Daisy as Boom lumbered toward her. "But I got involved in a photo shoot, so . . ."

It was only a few weeks since Daisy's encounter with the magical yellow butterfly, but she was already so used to talking to animals that it didn't seem the least bit strange to her. In fact, it would have seemed stranger if she'd suddenly discovered she *couldn't* talk to them.

"A photo shoot?" asked Boom. "What's that?"

"I got a new camera for my birthday, and I've been taking photos with it," said Daisy. Boom looked puzzled, so she tried to explain. "You know when you shut your eyes and, if you concentrate, you can still see someone's face for a while?"

Boom shut his eyes and nodded.

"Well," said Daisy, "a camera stops it from fading away. I'll show you tomorrow, if you like."

"I *would*," said Boom. Then he sniffed the air. "Have you been making jam sandwiches?"

"Oh, that's my new perfume," said Daisy. "Strawberry Surprise." She opened her lunch box and took out the ham sandwich she had made for him. "Would you prefer jam tomorrow?"

"No thanks," replied Boom, chomping on the sandwich. "Jam is fine, but ham is *divine*. Want some company?"

"Always," said Daisy. She opened the gate to let him out, and together they trotted down the lane.

"BUZZY-BUZZY JAM JAM,
BUZZY-BUZZY JAM JAM,
ME-WANT, ME-WANT, ME-WANT, ME-WANT!
BUZZY-BUZZY JAM JAM,
BUZZY-BUZZY JAM JAM,
ME-WANT, ME-WANT, ME-WANT, ME-WANT!"

"Aargh!" squealed Daisy, flapping her
arms around. "It's a wasp!"
"BUZZY-BUZZY JAM JAM,
BUZZY-BUZZY JAM JAM,
ME-WANT, ME-WANT, ME-WANT, ME-WANT!"

"Keep still," said Boom as the wasp circled above Daisy's head. "He'll fly away in a minute."

"But he's not flying away!" squeaked Daisy. "He keeps trying to land on me!"

"I think it's your perfume," said Boom. "Tell him."

"What?" asked Daisy, flapping frantically. "What do you mean, 'tell him'?"

"Just tell him he's wasting his time," said Boom.

"Oh," said Daisy. She fixed the wasp with a hard stare. "Now listen here," she said sternly. "I don't have anything for you to eat, so why don't you just buzz off?"

The wasp flew back a little way and hovered in front of her.

"BUZZY-WHAT? BUZZY-WHAT? BUZZY-WHAT? BUZZY-WHAT?"

"I'm *saying*," said Daisy, "that whatever you want, I don't have it."

"LIAR-BUZZ,
LIAR-BUZZ,
LIAR-BUZZ,
LIE!"

"I am *not* a
liar," said Daisy
irritably. "What you smell is my
strawberry perfume, that's all. You
can't eat it, so you might as well leave
me alone and go do something
useful instead."

"That'll be the day," said Boom.

The wasp changed direction and began buzzing angrily around Boom's head.

Boom yawned. "Why don't you just calm down for a minute and listen to what she's trying to tell you?"

The wasp settled on a fence post.

"BUT I SMELL IT, I SMELL IT, I SMELL IT, I SMELL IT!"

"I told you," Daisy explained, "it's my perfume. You *can't* eat it."

The wasp crawled around on top of the fence post, buzzing its wings impatiently.

"DON'T CARE, DON'T CARE, WANNIT, WANNIT, WANNIT, WANNIT!"

"I tell you what," said Daisy, taking out her lunch box. "I'll let you have some of my chocolate cookie if you promise to leave me alone."

"GIVE IT-WANNIT-GIVE IT-WANNIT-GIVE IT-WANNIT-GIVE IT-WANNIT!"

"I think," said Boom, "that's as close as you're going to get."

"All right," said Daisy, putting a small piece of chocolate on top of the fence post. "But a deal's a deal, remember."

"BUZZY-YUMMY, BUZZY-YUMMY, BUZZY-YUMMY, YUM-YUM!"

"I think he likes it," said Daisy as they walked away. "He was a bit rude, though, wasn't he? Not very well brought up."

"Ah," said Boom, "but think about that poor queen, having to lay eggs all day long. If you were a single mom with ten thousand kids, would you have time to teach them any manners?"

"That," said Daisy thoughtfully, "is a very good point."

Somewhere in the distance, a bell rang.

"Uh-oh. Speaking of chocolate, I think I'm going to be the end of it."

"Eh?" said Boom.

Daisy smiled. "Chock-oh-*late*."

She hitched up her backpack, kissed the top of his head, and ran off down the lane.

Boom watched her go for a few moments, then sat and stared at a small snail.

"I don't get it," he said.

Chapter 2
Late Again

When she reached her classroom, Daisy peered through a crack in the door and saw that Miss Frink's pen was poised above the attendance book. Why couldn't she have been called Daisy *Zinkleman*? At least then she'd have a chance of making it to her seat on time.

As it was, Miss Frink had done Kimberly Kibble and was already galloping toward Gareth Watkins and Abigail Wilson. To make matters worse, it was Quiet Reading Time,

and unless Bobby Mitchell fell off his chair
into the display of models from the class's
Design Your Own House project, there was
no way she would make it in unnoticed.

"Four legs, please, Bobby," said Miss
Frink, removing Daisy's last hope. "And
that doesn't include your own."

As Bobby's chair thumped back onto the
carpet, Daisy opened the door and strode
quickly to her place, hoping that no one
would notice.

"Good morning, Daisy," snapped Miss
Frink. "Or should I say *good afternoon*?"

Oh, dear, thought Daisy. *Caught again.*

"Good morning, Miss Frink," she said,
hooking her backback onto her chair. Jessica
Jenkins beamed at her from the next table,
but as Daisy smiled back, Miss Frink said,
"I hope you don't think this is funny, Daisy
Dawson."

"No, Miss Frink," said Daisy. "I don't think it's funny."

"Well, I do," said Furball the gerbil through the bars of his cage. "I *Frink* it's hilarious, actually."

"Stop it," Daisy told him sternly.

"And it's no good muttering under your breath either," Miss Frink went on. "It's time you got your act together, young lady. Next week, I want you here before the bell rings. Is that clear?"

"Yes, Miss Frink," said Daisy. She sat down and glared at Furball.

"Don't get mad at me," he said. "I was here in plenty of time."

"Yeah," said Burble, popping her head up next to him.

"Like you had a *choice*." She peered at Daisy through the bars. "Doing good, Daisy D?"

Daisy nodded and looked in Miss Frink's direction.

"Oh, right, got it. No can talk." Burble pretended to zip her mouth shut with her paw. "Catch you later, then."

Daisy gave a thumbs-up, then turned back to Miss Frink, who was now standing in front of the class. "All eyes this way, please."

Two little sucking noises came from the gerbils' cage, and Daisy saw that Furball was pretending to remove his eyeballs. She decided to ignore him.

"This morning we are going to start our research into habitats," said Miss Frink. "Who can tell me what a habitat is?"

Daisy thrust her hand up into the air, but Bobby Mitchell was there first, stretching his arm way out and shouting, "Ooh, ooh!"

"All right, Bobby,"
said Miss Frink. "Enlighten us."

"It's a furry thing," said Bobby. "A furry
thing that goes *meow*."

Everyone burst out laughing, including
Bobby. Although he wasn't sure what was
so funny, he liked that his answer had made
the whole class laugh.

"That's a tabby cat," said Miss Frink. "Now,
does anyone have a *sensible* suggestion?"

Puzzled, Bobby leaned back on his chair
and began chewing the end of his pencil.

"Daisy? Perhaps you can redeem yourself this morning?"

Daisy sat up straight and thought about the nature film they had watched last week.

"A habitat is a place where animals make their homes," she said.

"Good," said Miss Frink. "Can you give us an example?"

"Well," said Daisy, "rabbits live in fields, so that's their natural habitat and, um, squirrels live up trees, so that's their habitat."

"Excellent," said Miss Frink. "Those are two very good examples, Daisy. Now we are going to read about different habitats around the world. I want you all to make some notes, then later on I'll tell you about your special assignment for the weekend."

The library monitors had made a display of reference books at the side of the classroom, and Daisy's table was allowed to go up first and choose.

Daisy found a photograph of some gerbils in a sandy desert and sidled up to Burble and Furball's cage.

"Pssst!" she whispered. "You two! Come and look at this!"

The gerbils scampered over and stuck their noses through the bars. Daisy opened the book and showed them the picture.

"Wow!" said Furball. "Excellent!"

"Anyone we know?" asked Burble.

"That's your natural habitat," whispered Daisy. "It's where your ancestors came from."

"No way!" said Burble.

"Cool!" said Furball. "My grandpa was a surf dude!"

He began to do a little dance, twisting his feet in the sawdust and singing, *"Surf's up, sugar. Come 'n' surf it with me!"*

Daisy remembered how much he had enjoyed last semester's project on the seaside and decided she had better break it to him gently.

"It's not a beach, Furball," she explained. "It's a *desert*."

"Of course it's a beach," said Furball, continuing to dance around with his paws held out in front of him as if he were stirring with a large spoon. "Look at all the sand! Imagine that! Running down to the ocean every morning, catching a few waves and still making it back for breakfast. Surf-tastic!"

"It would have to be a very late breakfast," said Daisy. "The beach is about a thousand miles away."

"A thousand miles?" exclaimed Furball, stopping his dance. "A thousand *miles*?"

Burble cupped a paw to her ear. "Is it me, or is there an echo in here?"

"Like I said, it's a *desert* habitat," Daisy explained patiently. "That means lots of sun, lots of sand, but no ocean."

"Not even a tide pool?" Furball asked hopefully.

Daisy shook her head. "Nope."

"Well, I don't see the point of that," said Furball. "I'd rather live here, to be honest."

"That's lucky," said Burble.

"Got any Cheesy Whatsits?" asked Furball, changing the subject.

"I've got some in my lunch box," said Daisy. "I'll go and get you one."

"One?" said Furball.

"I was right," said Burble. "There *is* an echo in here."

Chapter 3
Hazel and Conker

On her way home from school that
afternoon, Daisy saw Meadowsweet
grazing in the farmer's field and stopped
to talk to her.

"Hello, my lovely," said Meadowsweet,
putting her head over the gate and nuzzling
Daisy's hair. "Did you had a nice day at
school?"

"Pretty good actually," said Daisy,
"although I was late again this morning."

"Oh, well," replied Meadowsweet.

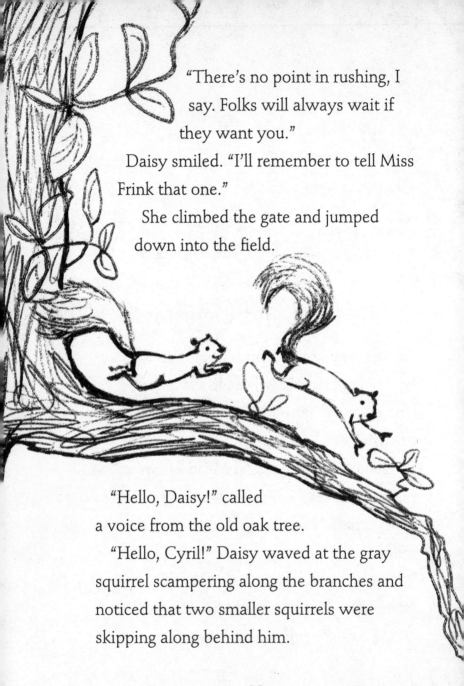

"There's no point in rushing, I
say. Folks will always wait if
they want you."

Daisy smiled. "I'll remember to tell Miss
Frink that one."

She climbed the gate and jumped
down into the field.

"Hello, Daisy!" called
a voice from the old oak tree.

"Hello, Cyril!" Daisy waved at the gray
squirrel scampering along the branches and
noticed that two smaller squirrels were
skipping along behind him.

28

"Who's Cyril got with him?" she asked.

"That's Hazel and Conker," said Meadowsweet. "They're his sister's children. Cyril's agreed to look after them while she visits friends in Leafscuffle Woods. I think he's beginning to regret it already."

Cyril bounded down the tree trunk and stopped next to the horse trough, closely followed by Hazel and Conker.

"Look!" exclaimed Conker, jumping up onto the edge of the trough. "A swimming pool! Can we go swimming, Uncle Cyril? Can we? Please? Can we?"

"No," said Cyril firmly. "Squirrels don't *go* swimming. Didn't your mother teach you anything?"

"Nope," said Conker cheerfully. "Does that mean I can go in?"

"No," said Cyril. "It does not."

"What if I *fell* in?"

"Accidentally on purpose you mean?"
Hazel giggled.

"All right, that's enough," said Cyril.
"Come on. Come down from there."

Daisy tried to keep a straight face as
Conker held out his arms and walked
unsteadily along the side of the trough, like
a tightrope walker in a high wind.

"Wibbly-wobbly, wibbly-wobbly . . ."

"Conker!" scolded Cyril.

As Conker jumped down and
somersaulted across the grass, Daisy
noticed that Hazel was staring at her.

"Hello," said Daisy. "You must be Hazel."

"Yes," replied Hazel shyly. "Are you Daisy? Uncle Cyril told us all about the Battle of Krackdown Kennels. About how he was a big brave hero and you helped him a tiny bit—"

"Yes, yes, yes," interrupted Cyril hurriedly. "I'm sure Daisy doesn't want to be reminded of all that again, do you, Daisy? I imagine you have some important business to attend to, eh?"

"Well, actually, I have a project to do this weekend," said Daisy. "We're supposed to find out about some animal habitats near where we live. I was wondering if I could come and take a few photos tomorrow."

"Photos?" piped up Conker. "What's photos?"

"You take them with a camera," Daisy explained. "You just go *click-click* and then you've got a picture to keep forever."

"Don't know what you're talking about," replied Conker, "but it sounds great."

"Can I take a picture of *you,* Daisy?" asked Hazel in a small voice.

Daisy crouched down and stroked Hazel's head. "Of course you can."

"Gosh," whispered Hazel. "Thanks, Daisy!" Then she ran around and hid behind Cyril.

At that moment a sleek gray cat emerged from the bushes, settled in a patch of warm sunlight, and regarded Daisy with cool green eyes. It was Trixie McDixie.

"So," purred Trixie, "you want to take some pictures."

"Yes," said Daisy. "I thought I'd take some of Cyril and Meadowsweet in their natural habitat."

"Hmm," said Trixie. "Don't want to be rude, but wouldn't you like to take pictures of something a little less . . . ordinary?"

"Hey!" protested Cyril. "I'm one-of-a-kind! I'm unique!"

"Can't argue with that," said Trixie. "Still . . ."

"What did you have in mind?" asked Daisy.

"Well, it just so happens that while I was out hunting in the woods last night, I heard a rumor that a pair of otters have moved in a few miles downriver. They keep to themselves of course, but it might be worth the trip just to get something . . . how shall I put this? . . . that isn't a squirrel."

"What's *wrong* with squirrels?" demanded Cyril.

"How long do you have?" purred Trixie.

"There's *nothing* wrong with squirrels," said Daisy hurriedly. "But it does sound exciting. We could have an expedition."

"An expedition!" exclaimed Cyril, cheering up immediately. "I could be team leader!"

"Oh, please," said Trixie. "Give me a break."

"Can we come?" chorused Hazel and Conker. "Can we, can we?"

"I don't know," said Cyril cautiously. "It could be highly dangerous." He looked pointedly in Conker's direction. "A mission such as this would be suitable only for *sensible* squirrels."

Conker immediately stood up straight and put his paws by his sides. "I can do sensible."

Hazel went cross-eyed behind Cyril's back

in an attempt to make Conker laugh. Conker sniggered, then stamped his foot and saluted. "Corporal Conker reporting for duty, sir!"

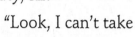

"Look, I can't take any more of this," said Trixie irritably. "If you're interested, Daisy, my advice is to ditch the squirrels and follow the river down past Darkwater Sump. Keep your wits about you and you should be able to find them."

"Wait!" said Daisy as Trixie disappeared into the bushes. "What's Darkwater Sump?"

"Darkwater Sump," said a familiar voice behind her, "is a deep hole which sucks water down beneath the riverbed."

"Boom!" Daisy reached out to pat him as he sat down beside her. "Are you coming on our expedition?"

"Of course," said Boom, "but we'll need to be careful. They say Darkwater Sump is a dangerous place for the unwary."

Daisy noticed that Cyril was sketching a map in the dust.

"All right, everyone," he announced. "Gather around!"

As they clustered around the map, Cyril used a twig to point out key objectives.

"Now, this," he said, "is our starting point, where we will assemble at 0900 hours, then proceed down the riverbank in an orderly fashion."

"Looks like a dandelion to me," said Hazel.

"Well it *is* a dandelion," replied Cyril wearily. "I'm trying to show you where things are, that's all. That's the whole point of a map. The dandelion is *irrelevant*."

"An elephant?" asked Hazel, at which point Conker burst out laughing and had to stuff a leaf in his mouth to muffle the sound.

"Look," snapped Cyril, "are you sure I can trust you to be sensible squirrels?"

"Pleeuhh!" said Conker, spitting out the leaf.

"Of course," said Hazel, stepping in front of him. "We're always sensible."

There was silence for a moment, followed by a tremendous splash. As everyone turned to look, Conker stuck his head out of the horse trough and grinned.

"Anyone care for a swim?"

Chapter 4
Daisy's Expedition

Daisy woke up early the next morning and began to pack the things she would need. She picked up her blue backpack and carefully put in her camera and a clean pair of socks, just in case. Then she found her raincoat at the back of the closet and stuffed it in on top. Although it looked as though it was going to be another bright, sunny day, there were one or two gray clouds on the horizon, and the lady on last night's weather forecast had said there could be sudden showers *almost anywhere*.

Daisy had been a Brownie, so she knew the importance of being prepared.

She tiptoed down into the kitchen and packed enough supplies to keep her and Boom going through what she guessed would be a long day. Extra-thick ham sandwiches, two packages of cheese-and-onion chips, and a couple of chocolate cookies, plus an extra one in case of emergency.

"Morning, Daisy," said Boom as Daisy climbed over the gate and patted Meadowsweet on the neck. "Figure we might get wet today."

"Do you think so?" asked Daisy, glancing up to see that the number of clouds on the horizon had somehow doubled since the last time she'd looked. But there was still plenty of blue sky around, so she decided

there wasn't
too much to worry about.
She watched Conker at the
top of the tree, dropping
acorns into the water
trough while Cyril tried
to explain something to
a bored-looking Hazel.

"Cyril's getting wet
already," Daisy said with
a grin.

"I don't mean to hurry you,"
interrupted Meadowsweet,
"but if you're going, it might
be best to make
an early start."

"Aren't you coming with us?" Daisy asked.

"I'm afraid not," said Meadowsweet. "The path is too narrow for me. But I'll be waiting right here until you're safely home."

Daisy looked around to see Hazel and Conker scampering across the field toward the woods, with Cyril chasing after them, shouting, "Wait! I'm the leader! Leader goes first!"

"Be careful, won't you?" said Meadowsweet.

But Daisy and Boom were already running to catch up with the others. Meadowsweet watched them until they reached the edge of the field: two tiny dots beneath a sky that was becoming darker and grayer with every second.

*　*　*

"This way, everyone!" called Cyril.

Daisy climbed the fence and scrambled down the riverbank. She kneeled on sun-dappled stones and splashed cool water on her face. Boom waited patiently, then waded slowly and carefully through the river beside her as she skipped across the stones to the other side.

They followed Cyril along the woodland path, the light tinged with green where sunshine filtered through the leaves.

"Halt!" shouted Cyril suddenly. "Everybody halt!"

Hazel and Conker staged a mini pile-up behind him, sending

Cyril sprawling into a patch of wild garlic.
He leaped to his feet, brushed bark from his
coat, and, staggering slightly, pointed to a
wire fence in front of them.

"That," he warned, "is an electric fence.
Whatever you do, do *not* touch it!"

"What's it for?" Daisy whispered.

"It marks the edge of the farmer's land,"
explained Boom. "Makes sure that any lost
sheep don't stray too far from home."

"Look," said Daisy, pointing down the
riverbank. "The fence stops at that tree.
How about we walk along the river until
we get past it?"

"We could," replied Boom, "but the river
comes right up to the tree."

"Oh, well," said Daisy. "We'll just have to
get wet."

"You're forgetting something," said Cyril.
"Squirrels can climb trees. In fact, climbing
trees is what we do best."

"Of course," said Daisy. "I didn't think of that."

She looked up at the big old beech tree and saw that even its lowest branches were too high for her to reach.

"I tell you what," she said. "You squirrels climb the tree and Boom and I will go the river way. Then we'll meet up on the other side."

"Dear me, no!" said Cyril. "That would never do. I couldn't possibly abandon members of my platoon. What if a shark attacked you? How would I live with myself?"

Daisy smiled. "Sharks don't live in rivers. It's not their natural habitat. A shark's natural habitat is the ocean."

"Ah," said Cyril knowingly, "but has anyone told *them* that?"

"Well . . ." said Daisy hesitantly.

Boom shook his head as if he couldn't believe what he was hearing.

"I tell you what," said Daisy. "If we see any sharks, we'll call you. Then you can distract them by throwing acorns or something."

"Shark-bombing with acorns," said Conker happily. "Hooray!"

"Won't that annoy them, though?" asked Hazel. "They might come up the tree and bite us."

"I didn't think of that," said Conker. He turned to Daisy. "Daisy, can sharks climb trees?"

"No," said Daisy, trying not to laugh as Boom put a paw over his eyes. "I think you're pretty safe up there."

"Excellent," said Conker, scampering excitedly toward the tree. "Come on, Haze. Those sharks better watch out!"

Boom shook his head again and said, "If that squirrel had any sense, he'd be dangerous."

Beneath the branches of a weeping willow tree, the river grew dark and spun around upon itself, like water disappearing down a drain.

"What is it?" Daisy whispered.

"That," said Boom, "is Darkwater Sump."

Gripping tightly onto a branch that grew above the river, Daisy planted one foot firmly in the center of the tree trunk and swung herself around until she hung suspended over the water.

"Steady, now!" warned Boom. "Don't fall!"

"Don't worry!" Daisy called back. "I'm all right!"

Still hanging onto the branch, she walked around the tree trunk until she was almost on the other side, then she pushed off with both feet and landed with a soft thump.

"Made it!" she exclaimed. She heard a faint pattering sound above her and looked up to see Hazel and Conker standing on the end of a branch, clapping their paws together. "Well done, Daisy!"

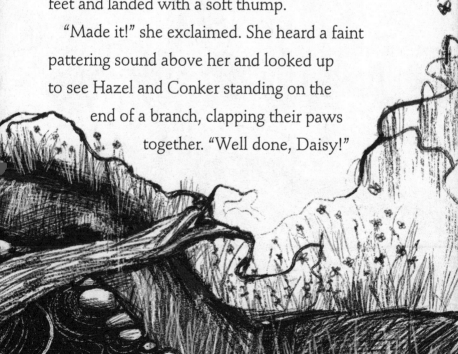

shouted Hazel. "You should have been
a squirrel!"

Daisy glanced back at Boom and
saw that he was looking worried.
"Are you all right, Boom?"

"Ye–es," said Boom uncertainly.
He looked up at the tree and
then back at the river.
"It's just . . . I don't know
if I can swim."

Daisy realized that, although he was
being brave, Boom was afraid of the fast-
flowing water.

"Here," she said, catching hold of the
branch again and swinging back to the
middle of the tree trunk. "Let me
help you."

She held on to the branch
with one hand and
stretched out the other
toward Boom. Boom
took one last look at
the water. Then, as he
scrabbled at the bank,
Daisy grabbed him by
the collar and hauled
him around to the other side.
"Yay!" cheered the squirrels as
Daisy jumped down next to Boom
and gave him a hug.

"Thanks for helping," he whispered.

Daisy pressed her cheek against his head. "That's what friends are for," she said.

"Right," announced Cyril. "We are now nearing our objective, so I suggest we keep communication to a minimum."

"What's he talking about?" asked Conker.

"I think he means we'd better be quiet," Daisy explained. "He doesn't want us to frighten the otters."

"Oh. Why didn't he say so then?"

"Code," said Hazel, tapping her nose. "Top-secret code."

They walked along the path in silence for a while. In the treetops, a bird sang a song about storms.

"Look," said Boom. "I think we're nearly there."

Ahead of them, the woods opened out into a deep meadow. The grass was

drenched with wildflowers: blue
cornflowers and yellow buttercups jostled
with pink campion and purple cranesbill.
A breath of wind sent a wave of color
rippling across the surface like a whisper.

"Oh," breathed Daisy. "It's beautiful!"

At a bend in the river, beneath a line of
willow trees, was a deep, shining pond.

In the middle of the pond, something
moved.

"Is that them?" she whispered. "Is that the
otters?"

"That's them, all right," said Boom. "But I
think they might be wary of you, Daisy. In
the past, humans have destroyed their
habitats. They've built houses, roads, and
factories in the places where otters used to
live. Sometimes they've even hunted them."

"That's terrible!" Daisy protested. "Why
would anyone do that?"

"I suppose," said Hazel, sitting on Daisy's shoe and gazing up at her, "it's because not everyone is as nice as you."

Daisy stroked the little squirrel's head and looked anxiously at Cyril.

"Does that mean the otters won't want to see me?"

"Well," said Cyril, taking charge again, "there's only one way to find out."

Chapter 5
Dampsy and Spray

When they reached the far side of
the meadow, Daisy pushed her way
through a curtain of willow branches and
stood on the riverbank, looking down into
the deep pond. There was a flash of blue as
a kingfisher flew across the surface before
disappearing into a clump of trees. But there
was no sign of the otters.

Cyril sat on a branch, swaying in the
breeze. "Can't see 'em," he said. "How
about you, Boom?"

Boom lifted his paw, and Daisy saw that he was pointing to a raft of branches. Beyond it, two pairs of eyes stared out from a hole in the riverbank.

"There they are!" whispered Hazel, hiding behind Daisy's leg. "Are they fierce?"

"No," Daisy reassured her, "but I imagine they're a little nervous. They don't know who we are."

"I'll go and have a word with them," said Cyril.

He scampered down the tree and ran along the bank until he came to the pile of branches. He skipped nimbly over the top, then stood on a log that was half submerged in the water and peered into the otters' den.

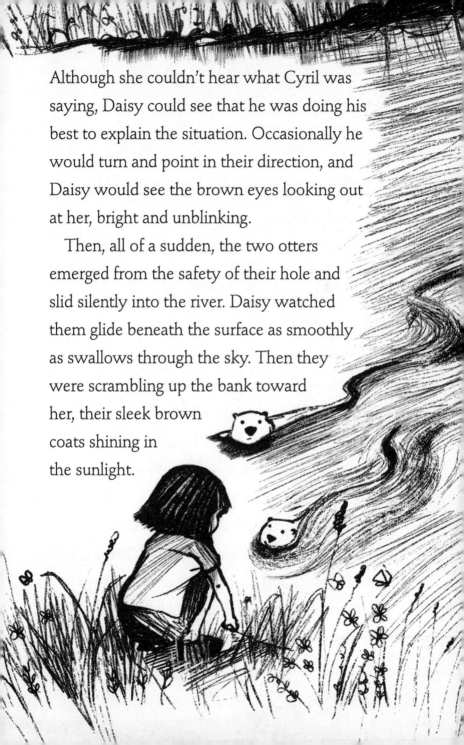

Although she couldn't hear what Cyril was
saying, Daisy could see that he was doing his
best to explain the situation. Occasionally he
would turn and point in their direction, and
Daisy would see the brown eyes looking out
at her, bright and unblinking.

Then, all of a sudden, the two otters
emerged from the safety of their hole and
slid silently into the river. Daisy watched
them glide beneath the surface as smoothly
as swallows through the sky. Then they
were scrambling up the bank toward
her, their sleek brown
coats shining in
the sunlight.

"Hello," said the smaller otter. "You must be Daisy."

"Yes," said Daisy shyly. "It's nice to meet you."

The otters turned to look at each other, then looked back at her again.

"So it's true," said the larger of the two. "You really can understand us!"

"Yes," said Daisy. "Does that seem strange?"

"Well, dear," said the smaller otter, "it's not every day we have a conversation with a real, live girl. Is it, Spray?"

"No," said Spray, and Daisy could tell that he was still a bit suspicious of her. "The world is full of surprises."

"I'm Dampsy, by the way," said the smaller otter, "and this is Spray." She winked at Daisy. "He'll cheer up once he realizes you're not going to steal his fish."

"It's not the fish I'm worried

about," said Spray. "She's a human, isn't she? How do we know we can trust her?"

"Oh, *really,* Spray!" Dampsy tutted and shook her head. "Look at her. You can see it in her eyes. She'd never hurt us in a million years!"

Spray studied Daisy for a moment and nodded. "I guess you're right. But what if she tells the others where we are? They'll come with their big machines, and that'll be the end of us."

"I won't tell anyone," promised Daisy. "I just want to take some pictures, that's all."

She took the camera from around her neck and showed them the pictures she had already taken.

Their eyes widened in disbelief as she showed them the photographs of Hazel and Conker playing in the water trough.

"I never knew such things existed!" gasped Dampsy. "Water squirrels, indeed!"

"Silly squirrels is more like it," muttered Cyril.

"Can you make pictures of us, too?" asked Dampsy.

"Of course," said Daisy. "Maybe I could take some over by your house. Would that be all right?"

"House?" Spray looked puzzled.

"She means our den," explained Dampsy. "Don't you, dear?"

"Can't see that it can hurt. Follow me," said Spray. He slid back into the river, and Dampsy joined him, disappearing beneath the surface with a *plop*.

"Well done, Daisy," said Boom as they

watched the two otters swim back toward their den. "I think you've won them over."

"They weren't frightening at all," said Hazel, emerging from her hiding place behind Daisy's leg.

"Do you want to come?" asked Daisy.

Hazel stared at the ground for a moment as if trying to remember something she had forgotten. "Umm . . ." she said. "Ummm . . ."

"I wonder," said Boom in a kind voice, "if anyone will stay here and keep me company."

"I will!" cried Hazel, sounding relieved. "If Daisy doesn't mind, that is."

Daisy smiled. "Of course not. You stay here with Boom. Cyril and Conker can pick some berries, and I'll get a few pictures. Then we'll all have lunch. Does that sound like a good plan?"

"It does," said Cyril. "In fact, I was just about to suggest it myself."

*   *   *

"Sorry about the mess," said Dampsy, sweeping some old fish heads beneath a branch with her paw. If I'd known you were coming I'd have cleaned up a bit."

"Don't worry," said Daisy. "It's a lovely den."

"Now then, young Daisy," said Spray. "Where would you like us?"

Daisy held up the camera. The two otters were framed in the viewfinder with the entrance to the den behind them. "Hold it there!" she said, pressing the button. "You look great!"

After she had taken a few pictures of them in the water, the otters climbed out to see the results.

"Oh, *my*!" exclaimed Dampsy. "Look, Spray, that's us. Swimming up and down in our own little pond!"

"That's a very fine job, Daisy," said Spray. "A very fine job indeed."

Daisy flushed pink with happiness.

"You must be hot and sticky after your journey," said Dampsy. "Why don't you come for a swim?"

Daisy looked down into the deep, clear water. It looked cool and inviting. "Really?" she asked. "Do you think I could?"

"Why not?" said Spray. "As the old saying goes, 'The day gets better as we all get wetter.'"

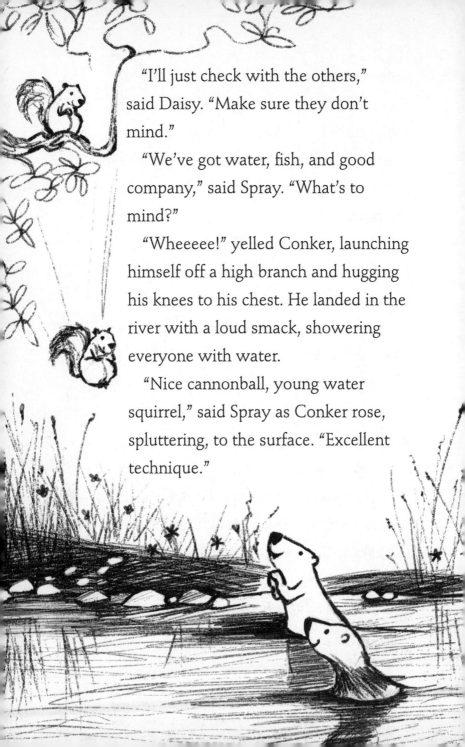

"I'll just check with the others," said Daisy. "Make sure they don't mind."

"We've got water, fish, and good company," said Spray. "What's to mind?"

"Wheeeee!" yelled Conker, launching himself off a high branch and hugging his knees to his chest. He landed in the river with a loud smack, showering everyone with water.

"Nice cannonball, young water squirrel," said Spray as Conker rose, spluttering, to the surface. "Excellent technique."

There was another splash as Hazel, who had quickly overcome her shyness, landed in the water next to him. Daisy could see her little paws scrabbling around on the riverbed before she pushed herself off and broke through the surface with a high-pitched squeak. She paddled her way toward the shallows and began splashing water at Cyril, who was supervising from the bank.

Boom was stretched out on the grass, watching with amusement.

"Aren't you coming in?" called Daisy, standing waist deep in the cool, refreshing water.

Boom shook his head. "Someone needs to guard the sandwiches."

Dampsy popped her head out of the water and tapped Daisy on the arm. "Come and swim with us!"

"I'm not very good at swimming underwater," said Daisy.

"But it's easy,"
said Dampsy. "Just
hold your breath,
open your eyes,
and follow me."

"Well . . . OK."

Daisy had never
opened her eyes
underwater before,
but now seemed like a good time to start.

She took a deep breath, flicked her feet
up, and tumbled beneath the surface, her
hair streaming behind her in the water. Her
eyes went blurry at first, but after a few
seconds everything became clear. She could
see the otters ahead of her, twisting through
duckweed, snuffling under stones, and
turning every now and then to check that
she was following.

Daisy pulled back her arms and kicked

her feet, wriggling over fallen branches and touching the shiny pebbles that lay on the riverbed beneath her. Soon she had caught up with them.

As Spray chased a stickleback downriver, Dampsy pointed to a water beetle paddling along the bottom. She swam down until her nose was almost touching it, then formed her mouth into an O, and, with a puff of her cheeks, blew a silver bubble of air, which enveloped the beetle before wobbling and shimmering up to the surface in a pool of light. This made Daisy laugh so much that she swallowed some water and had to swim up to the surface, chuckling and spluttering her way back to the bank.

"These are the best ever," said Boom, wolfing down a ham sandwich. "What did you do, Daisy, sprinkle them with magic?"

"French mustard actually," said Daisy. "Gives them that extra tang."

"Tang!" repeated Conker, flicking the back of Hazel's head. "You're it!"

"Doesn't count," said Hazel through a mouthful of strawberries. "My legs were crossed."

"Since when was that the rule?"

"Since you started saying *tang* and whacking me on the back of the head," replied Hazel.

"Oh," said Conker. "Fair enough."

"If I might interrupt for a moment," said Cyril, holding up a paw, "I think we can safely say: mission accomplished. All agreed?"

"Absolutely," said Daisy, offering a chip to Dampsy, who shook her head and patted her

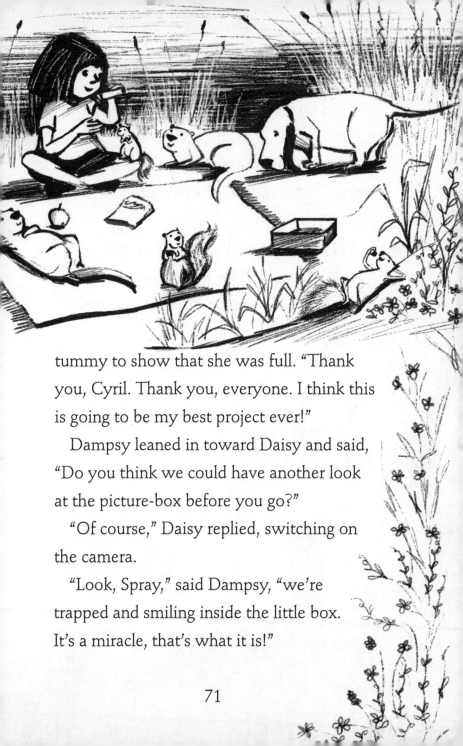

tummy to show that she was full. "Thank you, Cyril. Thank you, everyone. I think this is going to be my best project ever!"

Dampsy leaned in toward Daisy and said, "Do you think we could have another look at the picture-box before you go?"

"Of course," Daisy replied, switching on the camera.

"Look, Spray," said Dampsy, "we're trapped and smiling inside the little box. It's a miracle, that's what it is!"

71

"Yes, it is," said Spray.

"Let's take one last picture," said Daisy. "Of all of us."

She put the camera on an old tree stump, set the timer, and then ran back to join the others.

As the shutter clicked, Dampsy said, "There, now. One day you'll look in this magic box and remember the time you swam with us in the river."

"I won't need to," replied Daisy, "because today is a day I will never forget."

Chapter 6
Darkwater Sump

Daisy had been having such a good time
that she had completely forgotten about the
weather. But when she looked at the sky,
she saw dark thunderclouds stacked
overhead. The wind was picking up, and
the air smelled of rain.

"I hate to break up the party," said Boom,
"but I think we should be heading back.
There's a storm coming."

"Thank you so much for having us," said
Daisy. "It's been a wonderful afternoon."

"Come back and see us," said Dampsy, patting Hazel's arm. "Spray will catch some extra fish to celebrate, won't you, dear?"

"Of course," said Spray, ruffling the fur on top of Conker's head.

There were damp hugs all around, and then Daisy was running back through the meadow with the others. She climbed the stile and jumped down into the shade of the trees just as the heavens opened and the rain began to fall.

"Stay close, small squirrels!" shouted Cyril as thick water droplets tore through the leaves and splashed down onto the woodland floor.

"The day gets better as we all get wetter!" sang Conker, echoing Spray's words as he danced his way along the winding path. But Daisy could see that Boom was worried.

"What is it?" she asked. "What's the matter?"

Boom shook himself, sending droplets of water pattering off into the undergrowth. "All this rain," he said softly, "will make the river angry."

Daisy stroked his head. "Don't worry, Boom. When we get to the tree trunk, I'll hold on tight and I won't let you go. OK?"

Boom nodded. "OK," he said.

When they reached the tree-crossing, Cyril turned to Hazel and Conker, who were having a grand time splashing in the muddy puddles.

"Go on," he said. "Up you go."

As the squirrels scampered up the tree, Daisy looked down and saw that the water was rising higher and higher. The river seemed moody and mysterious now, very different from how it had felt when they'd swum in it only minutes before.

Daisy pushed her hair out of her eyes,

grabbed hold of the branch, and swung
out over the river. She wriggled around,
her toes splashing the surface, and saw her
reflection in the dark water below. Then
she thumped both feet against the tree
trunk, grabbed Boom's collar, and hauled
him across to safety.

She jumped down next to him and did a
little dance in the rain.

"We did it! We did it! We did it, Boom. We did it!"

Boom nodded his head in time with the rhythm, but Daisy could tell that his heart wasn't really in it. All he wanted was to be back in the old barn again, safe and warm and dry.

"OK, Boom." She laughed. "I've stopped dancing. We can go home now."

At that moment there was a little cry, followed by a faint splash. Daisy spun around and saw that Hazel had fallen from the tree and was desperately trying to swim toward the bank. But the current was too strong. It was pulling her down toward Darkwater Sump.

"Hazel!" cried Daisy, running to the water's edge.

"Wait!" Boom barked.

Without stopping to think, Daisy kicked off her shoes and threw herself headlong into the river.

"No!" Boom howled. *"Noooo!"*

The water was cold, and Daisy gasped as she swam forward, desperate to reach Hazel before the current took her away. She looked around frantically, but there was no sign of Hazel, and the current was much stronger here than it had been in the otters' pond. Daisy felt herself being pulled toward the whirlpool that swirled beneath the weeping willows, and she knew that it would drag her down into Darkwater Sump.

"Help!" she cried. "Help me, please!"

At that moment, a wet, bedraggled head appeared in the water next to her.

"Boom!" she gasped. *"Boom!"*

"Hang on to my neck,"
he instructed, "and don't let go."

Daisy did as she was told. As Boom
swam, she felt the powerful sweep of his
paws, paddling against the current that
had almost carried her away. When they
scrambled back onto the bank, Daisy
remembered why she had jumped into
the river in the first place.

"Hazel!" she called, turning to scan the
river and the willows and the dark water
beneath them. "Oh, Hazel, where *are* you?"

They all stared at the place where Hazel had been only a few moments before. Cyril shook his head, whispering, "It's all my fault. It's all my fault."

"No," said Daisy, close to tears. "It's not your fault, Cyril. It's no one's fault."

"Yes, it is," replied Cyril miserably. "I said this mission was too dangerous. I told them they shouldn't come. But I gave in, didn't I? I gave in when I should have said no."

Cyril put his head in his paws, and Conker started to cry. Daisy bit her lip and looked up at the sky. If only she'd listened to Meadowsweet's warning, or told someone at home about her plan. She hadn't thought carefully about how dangerous this day could be. They should never have come this far alone.

The storm was over now, and the only sound was raindrops falling

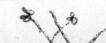

from the leaves, pattering gently down onto the woodland floor.

"What will I tell her mother?" Cyril muttered. "What will I tell her?"

"Tell her she needs some swimming lessons," said a gruff voice behind them. "And a cup of hot chamomile tea wouldn't be a bad idea."

They all turned to see a wet and thoroughly miserable-looking squirrel shivering beneath the dripping branches of a beech tree. Standing next to her was Spray.

Daisy's eyes widened, and Boom's mouth dropped open in disbelief.

"Hazel!" everyone cried.

Cyril ran and scooped her up in his arms while Conker danced around shouting, "She's alive! Hazel's alive!" at the top of his lungs.

"When she saw the storm coming," explained Spray, "Dampsy told me to swim up and check that you folks were all right. And"—here he nodded in Hazel's direction and winked at Daisy—"as usual, it looks like the missus was right."

Chapter 7
Daisy's Picture

"Have you finished your project?" asked
Boom as they ambled down the lane on
Monday morning.

"Yup," said Daisy, patting her backpack.
"Mission accomplished, as Cyril would say."

Boom chuckled. "It was a good day after
all, wasn't it?"

"The best," said Daisy.

They walked on in silence for a while.
Then Daisy stopped. She tucked a stray
wisp of hair behind her ear. "Boom," she

83

said. "There's something I've been meaning to ask you."

"Oh, yes?" said Boom. "And what might that be?"

Daisy looked at him thoughtfully. "Well, I don't mean to be rude or anything, but I sort of got the impression that you didn't like water very much. That you might even be a little bit scared of it. Is that true?"

"Yes," Boom admitted in a quiet voice. "I fell in the river once when I was a puppy. I nearly drowned. I've been scared of water ever since."

"But I don't understand," said Daisy. "In that case, how come you jumped in and saved me?"

Boom scratched at the ground with his paw and said nothing. In the distance, Daisy could hear the school bell ringing.

"Boom?" she asked again. "How come you saved me if you were so scared?"

Boom stopped scratching and looked up at her shyly.

"Because," he said, "the thought of losing you scared me even more."

As Daisy hugged him and then ran toward the school gates, Boom thought about the picture that she'd printed out that morning. She'd asked Cyril to take it to the otters, to say thank you for a wonderful day and for saving Hazel's life.

Walking back up the lane, listening to the bees buzz lazily among the foxgloves,

Boom thought of the men who would
come to the river one day, arriving with
their bulldozers to build factories, roads,
and houses.

He imagined them in years to come,
digging up the earth and branches of an
abandoned otters' den and scratching their
heads as they looked down at an old, faded
photograph.

A photograph of three squirrels, two
otters, and a dog.

And a little girl with wet hair and her
arms around them all, smiling in the light of
a golden afternoon.

WHEN A LAMB GOES MISSING, IT'S UP TO DAISY
AND HER ANIMAL FRIENDS TO FIND HIM.

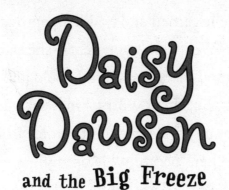

Daisy Dawson

and the Big Freeze

Steve Voake
illustrated by Jessica Meserve

A large ewe turned and eyed Daisy suspiciously.

"Hello," said Daisy, holding out her hand.
She quickly dropped it again when she realized
that trying to shake hands with a sheep was
probably not the best approach. "I'm Daisy
Dawson and I'm very pleased to meet you."

Shirelle looked at Boom. "Am I hearing
things," she asked, "or did the little two-
leggedy say she was pleased to meet me?"

"Daisy can talk to all of us," explained Boom

in his deep, quiet voice. "And what's more, she can understand what we're saying too."

Shirelle turned and nodded approvingly at Daisy. "Well, aren't you dear?" she said. "And such good manners. Ooh, I could just eat you up. But don't worry, I'm a vegetarian."

"Mommy!" bleated a little voice from behind her. "Mommy! Mommy!"

"Excuse me," said Shirelle, turning to look at the little white lamb struggling through the snow toward her. "What

an excerpt from *Daisy Dawson and the Big Freeze*

is it, Lillian my lambkin? What's the trouble?"

"It's Woolverton," said Lillian in a small, wavery voice. "He's wandered off again."

"Oh *no!*" said Shirelle. "Didn't I just tell him to stay with us?" She trotted over to where the lambs were gathered and stared out across the snowy fields.

"Is that him?" Daisy whispered as a dark shape came bounding across the snow.

"No," said Boom. "That's Ricky Round-Up." Daisy saw that it was a young sheepdog. "I know where he is, I know where he is," he panted.

JOIN DAISY DAWSON ON HER OTHER ANIMAL ADVENTURES!

www.candlewick.com